"Sometimes Thir

Being a mom is something special, even if she doesn't know it.
She's more than just your friend, she's your safety net.

Whenever you're in a bind, she's there to lend a hand,
Guiding you through life, helping you understand.

Through the highs and lows, she's your rock and your guide.
Like a lioness, she's fierce, always by your side.

She says, "Stay strong, stay positive and don't you dare give up,"
Encouraging you to stand tall, to always strive to win.

Heart-to-heart chats when you're feeling low,
Moms are like superheroes, their love will always show.

A praiser, a helper, an encourager too,
There's nothing in this world that she wouldn't do.

So here's a big thank you to all the moms out there,
For all that you do, for showing how much you care.

XOXO,
Daryl

Mami Is Raising a King!

Written By Daryl Antonio Rejas, Jr with Sally Rejas

Dedicated to all the mothers raising sons, and to the camels who often go unrecognized for their love and sacrifice.

Mami began reading a story to me, "Once upon a star, there was a starfish with only four legs."

But as I listened, a question stirred within me. I had to ask. "From the beginning of time, camels have stood by humans, sacrificing silently. Why do all stories begin with 'once upon a star'? Shouldn't it be 'Once Upon a Camel'?"

Mami, always patient with my questions, offered a wise response. "Camels are like all mothers, my dear. We don't seek recognition; we carry our responsibilities with humility and honor. You see, the responsibilities camels carry are often beyond words."

Her words drifted through my mind as she continued the story. Stars, camels, and mami's ran through my mind.

I admired Mami deeply. She was always there, offering guidance, discipline, and unconditional love. Her strength mirrored that of the camel, steadfast in her journey of love and sacrifice. Like the camel, she worked tirelessly to instill values of compassion, integrity, and patience in me.

Our bond, thrived on trust and understanding. Communication flowed effortlessly between us, whether through spoken words, subtle body language, or comforting touch.

Mami stood by me as my unwavering guardian, fiercely protecting me from the world's dangers. She is determined to nurture my growth, acting as my shield and keeping me safe.

As a future king, I learned vital skills from Mami. I learned how to find food. I learned to recognize dangers. I learned to handle social interactions. Her role in my development and survival was essential. It deserved recognition and gratitude. Just like a star.

Yet, Mami was more than a caretaker; she was my queen, nurturing me into the person I was destined to become— a king in my own right.

The End

About the Author

"I used to believe it was just me against the vast world, but then
I came to understand it was actually me against myself."

-Daryl Rejas Jr.

Daryl grew up in Virginia, Alabama, Maryland, and Georgia
as a military child. His passion has been animals, soccer,
creative writing & drama, and being outdoors.

After years of moving, Daryl has learned much in the moving
process and being a military child. One of the most important
lessons he has and continues to learn is how to fit in. In this
book and other platforms, his commitment is to stop bullying
and raise mental health awareness amongst young boys.
Daryl wants to talk about the elephant in the room and how
to mitigate those stressors.

"Whether things are big or small, whether we're feeling weak or strong, life is always changing. It's like stepping into a river - each time you do, it's not exactly the same river, and you're never exactly the same person."

-Daryl Rejas Jr.

Made in United States
Orlando, FL
14 September 2024

51510946R00015